For Marje, Pat, and Grace, librarians and friends
D. M.

For Jacob, Jesse, and Elieanna — great kids with bellybuttons
R. C.

Text copyright © 2005 by David Martin
Illustrations copyright © 2005 by Randy Cecil

First edition 2005

Library of Congress Cataloging-in-Publication Data

Martin, David, date.
We've All Got Bellybuttons! / David Martin ; illustrated by Randy Cecil. —1st ed.
p.   cm.
Summary: Various animals invite the reader to experience what their different
body parts can do, including their tickly belly buttons.
ISBN 0-7636-1775-X
[1. Bellybutton—Fiction. 2. Anatomy—Fiction. 3. Animals—Fiction.
4. Stories in rhyme.] I. Cecil, Randy, ill. II. Title.

PZ8.3.M4185We 2005
[E]—dc22   2004045904

2 4 6 8 10 9 7 5 3 1

Printed in China

This book was typeset in Clichee.
The illustrations were done in oil.

Candlewick Press
2067 Massachusetts Avenue
Cambridge, Massachusetts 02140

visit us at www.candlewick.com

We've All Got Bellybuttons!

David Martin

illustrated by Randy Cecil

CANDLEWICK PRESS

CAMBRIDGE, MASSACHUSETTS

We've got ears, and you do too.

We can pull them.

Can you?

We've got hands, and you do too.
We can clap them.

Can you?

We've got necks, and you do too.

We can stretch them.

We've got feet, and you do too.

We can kick them.

Can you?

We've got eyes,
and you do too.

We can close them.

Can you?

We've got mouths, and you do too.

We can open them.

Can you?

And we've all got bellybuttons,

and you do too.

And when they're tickle, tickle,

tickled . . .